# Harry Potter

## POSTER BOOK

# HOGWARTS
### THROUGH THE YEARS

# Harry Potter

## Poster Book

## Hogwarts
### THROUGH THE YEARS

SCHOLASTIC INC.
NEW YORK · TORONTO · LONDON · AUCKLAND · SYDNEY
MEXICO CITY · NEW DELHI · HONG KONG · BUENOS AIRES

ISBN 13: 978-0-545-03033-5
ISBN 10: 0-545-03033-1

Art Direction by Rick DeMonico
Interior designed by Two Red Shoes Design
Special Thanks to Henry Ng for his design expertise

12 11 10 9 8 7 6 5 4 3 2 1            7 8 9/0

Printed in Mexico
First printing, June 2007

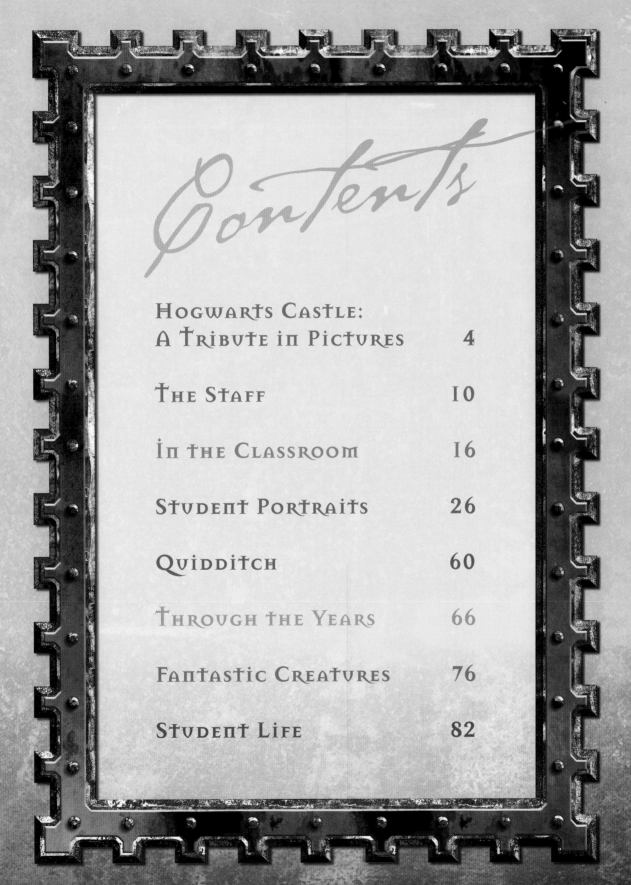

# Contents

# Hogwarts Castle:
## A Tribute in Pictures

4

THE HOGWARTS EXPRESS

THE GREAT HALL

Hogwarts Castle

THE CHAMBER OF SECRETS

THE FAT LADY — entrance to Gryffindor Tower

THE GRYFFINDOR COMMON ROOM

HOGWARTS CORRIDORS AND STAIRCASES

## The Hospital Wing

## Potions classroom

*Hogwarts Castle*

## The Owlery

## The Library

The Whomping Willow

Hagrid's hut

The Slytherin common room

The Staff

ALBUS DUMBLEDORE
Headmaster

## MINERVA McGONAGALL
DEPUTY HEADMISTRESS,
TRANSFIGURATION TEACHER,
HEAD OF GRYFFINDOR HOUSE

## RUBEUS HAGRID
KEEPER OF KEYS AND GROUNDS
AND CARE OF MAGICAL
CREATURES TEACHER

## SEVERUS SNAPE
POTIONS MASTER AND
HEAD OF SLYTHERIN HOUSE

## FILIUS FLITWICK
CHARMS TEACHER AND
HEAD OF RAVENCLAW HOUSE

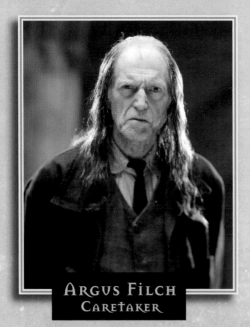

**ARGUS FILCH**
Caretaker

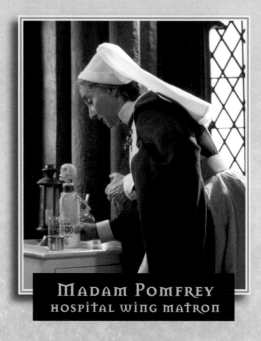

**MADAM POMFREY**
hospital wing matron

*The Staff*

**SIBYLL TRELAWNEY**
Divination teacher

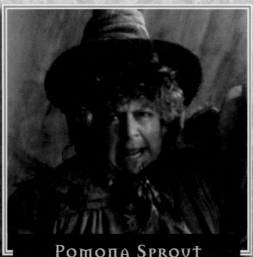

**POMONA SPROUT**
HERBOLOGY TEACHER AND
HEAD OF HUFFLEPUFF HOUSE

**MADAM HOOCH**
Quidditch teacher

# Defense Against the Dark Arts Teachers

**QUIRINUS QUIRRELL**
Year One

**GILDEROY LOCKHART**
Year Two

The Stage

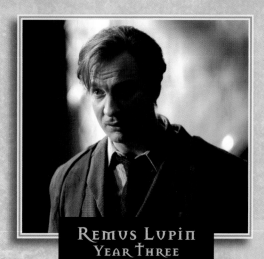

**REMUS LUPIN**
Year Three

**ALASTOR "MAD-EYE" MOODY**
Year Four

**DOLORES UMBRIDGE**
Year Five

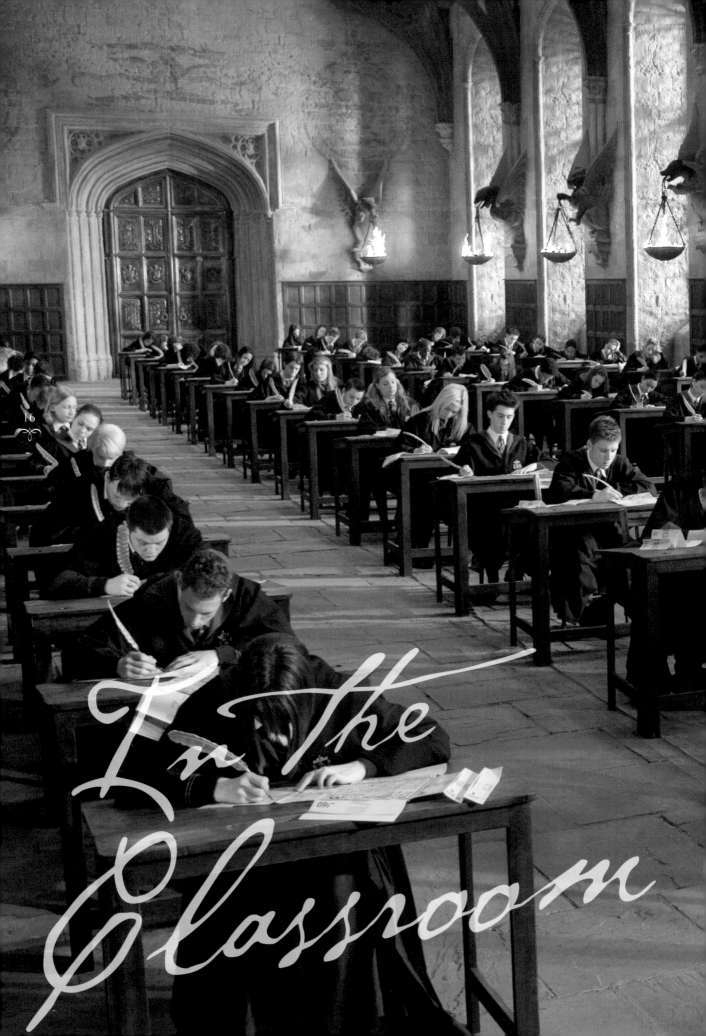

In The
Classroom

In the Classroom

19

In the Classroom

# Year Three

In the Classroom

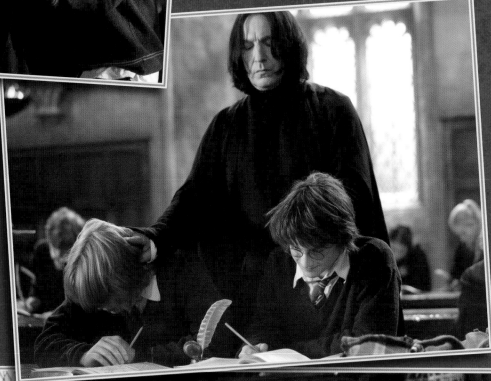

In the Classroom

In The Classroom

# Student Portraits

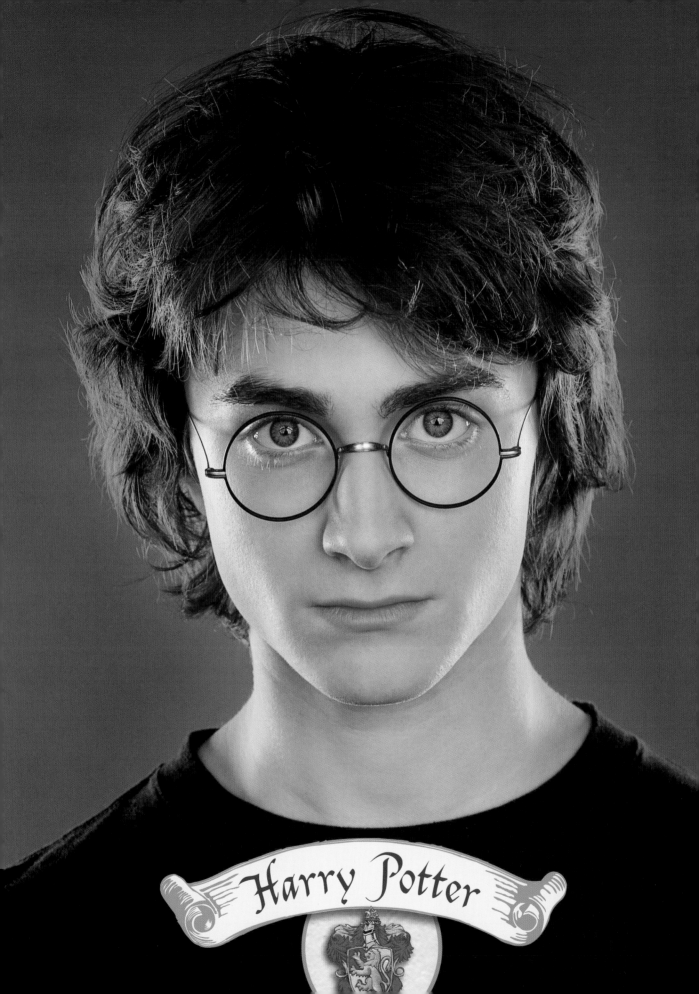

Harry Potter

Student Portraits

33

Student Portraits

Hermione Granger

GRYFFINDOR

Student Portraits

Student Portraits

Ron Weasley

Student Portraits

Student Portraits

Fred and George Weasley

Student Portraits

Student Portraits

Ginny Weasley

GRYFFINDOR

Neville Longbottom

GRYFFINDOR

Student Portraits

Seamus Finnigan

GRYFFINDOR

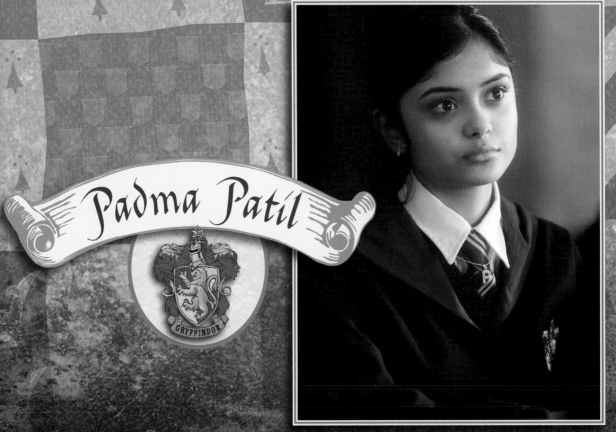

Padma Patil

GRYFFINDOR

## Parvati Patil

## Dean Thomas

Draco Malfoy

Student Portraits

Student Portraits

Vincent Crabbe

SLYTHERIN

Gregory Goyle

SLYTHERIN

Cedric Diggory

HUFFLEPUFF

Cho Chang

RAVENCLAW

# Luna Lovegood

RAVENCLAW

Student Portrait

Quidditch

Quidditch

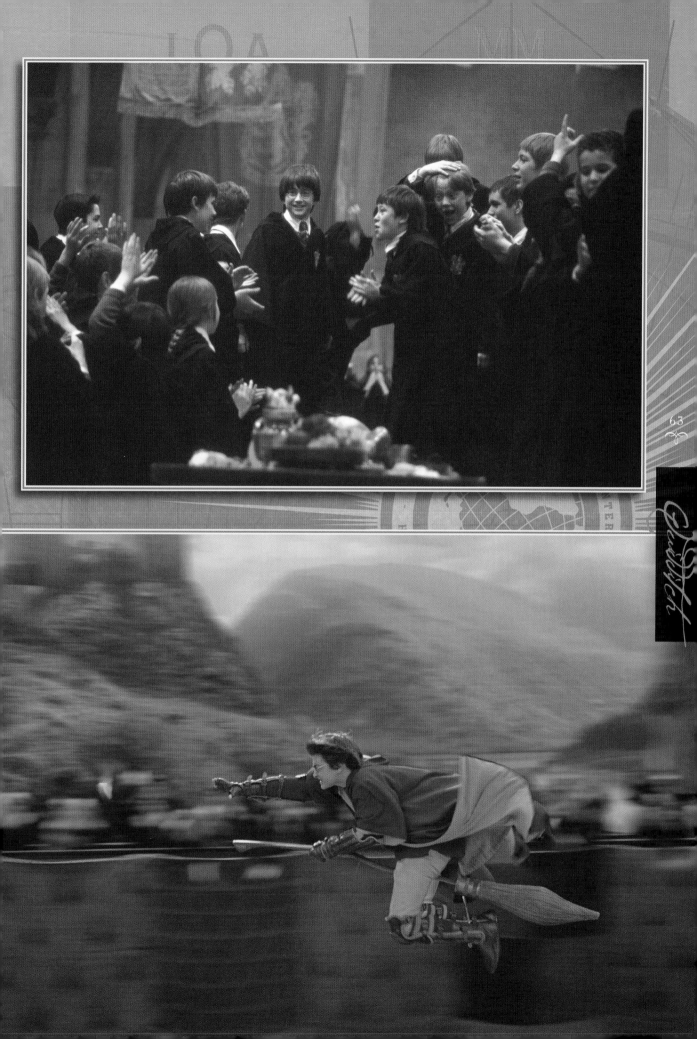

Through the Years

Through the Years

Through the Years

Through the Years

*Through the Years*

# Fantastic Creatures

FAWKES THE PHOENIX

BASILISK

Fantastic Creatures

DOBBY THE HOUSE-ELF

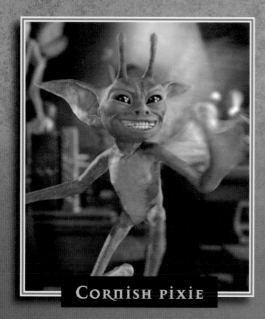

CORNISH PIXIE

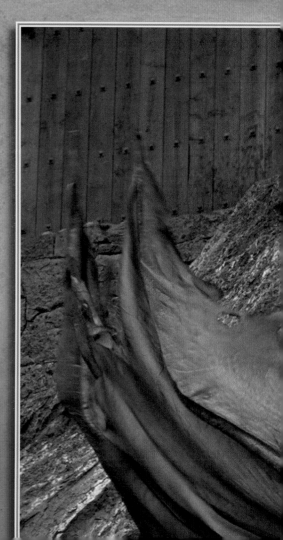

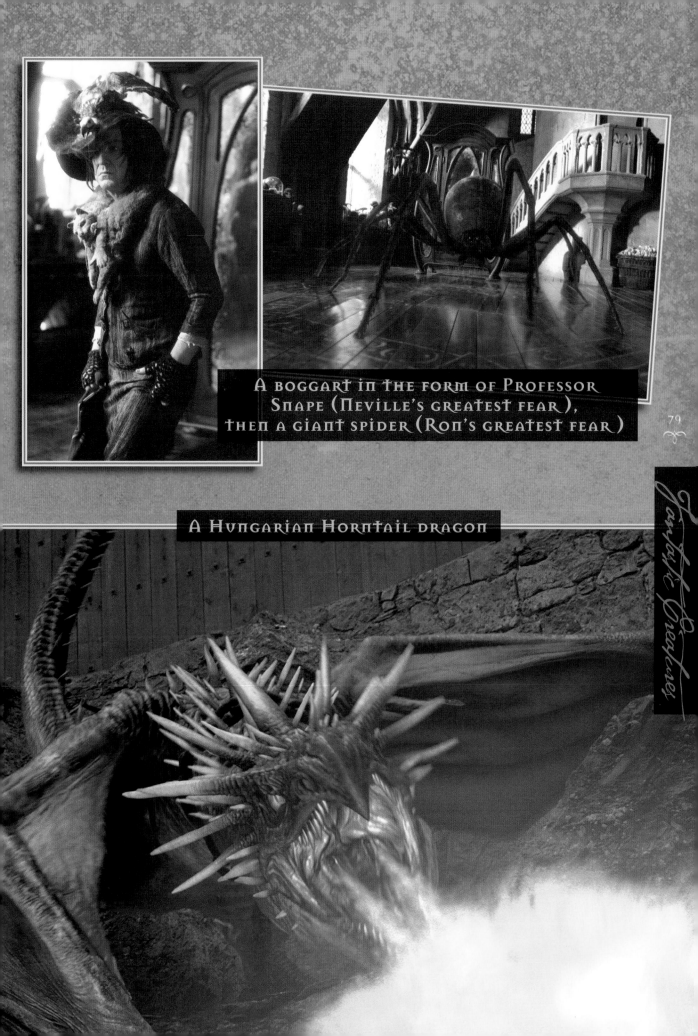

A boggart in the form of Professor Snape (Neville's greatest fear), then a giant spider (Ron's greatest fear)

A Hungarian Horntail dragon

Fantastic Creatures

Dementor

Sirivs Black in Animagvs form

Werewolf

Mermaid

Centaur

Thestral

Buckbeak the hippogriff

Goblin

Fantastic Creatures

Student Life

# Student Organizations

Student Life

### The Dueling Club

### Professor Umbridge's Inquisitorial Squad

### The school choir performs in the Great Hall.

# The Triwizard Tournament

THE FIRST TASK

AN IMPORTANT CLUE TO
THE SECOND TASK

THE GOBLET OF FIRE

AFTER THE SECOND TASK

Durmstrang champion
Viktor Krum

Beauxbatons champion
Fleur Delacour

The third task

Hogwarts champions Harry Potter
and Cedric Diggory

# The Yule Ball